Super Cuties

A Cosy Colouring Book About Love

by Rosie Bay

DK

Illustrated by Rosie Bay

First published in Great Britain in 2026 by
Dorling Kindersley Limited
20 Vauxhall Bridge Road,
London SW1V 2SA

The authorised representative in the EEA is
Dorling Kindersley Verlag GmbH. Arnulfstr. 124,
80636 Munich, Germany

10 9 8 7 6 5 4 3 2 1
001–354662–Jan/2026

A CIP catalogue record for this book is available from the British Library.
ISBN: 978-0-2417-7575-2

Printed and bound in China

www.dk.com

MIX
Paper | Supporting responsible forestry
FSC™ C018179

This book was made with Forest Stewardship Council™ certified paper – one small step in DK's commitment to a sustainable future.
Learn more at www.dk.com/uk/information/sustainability

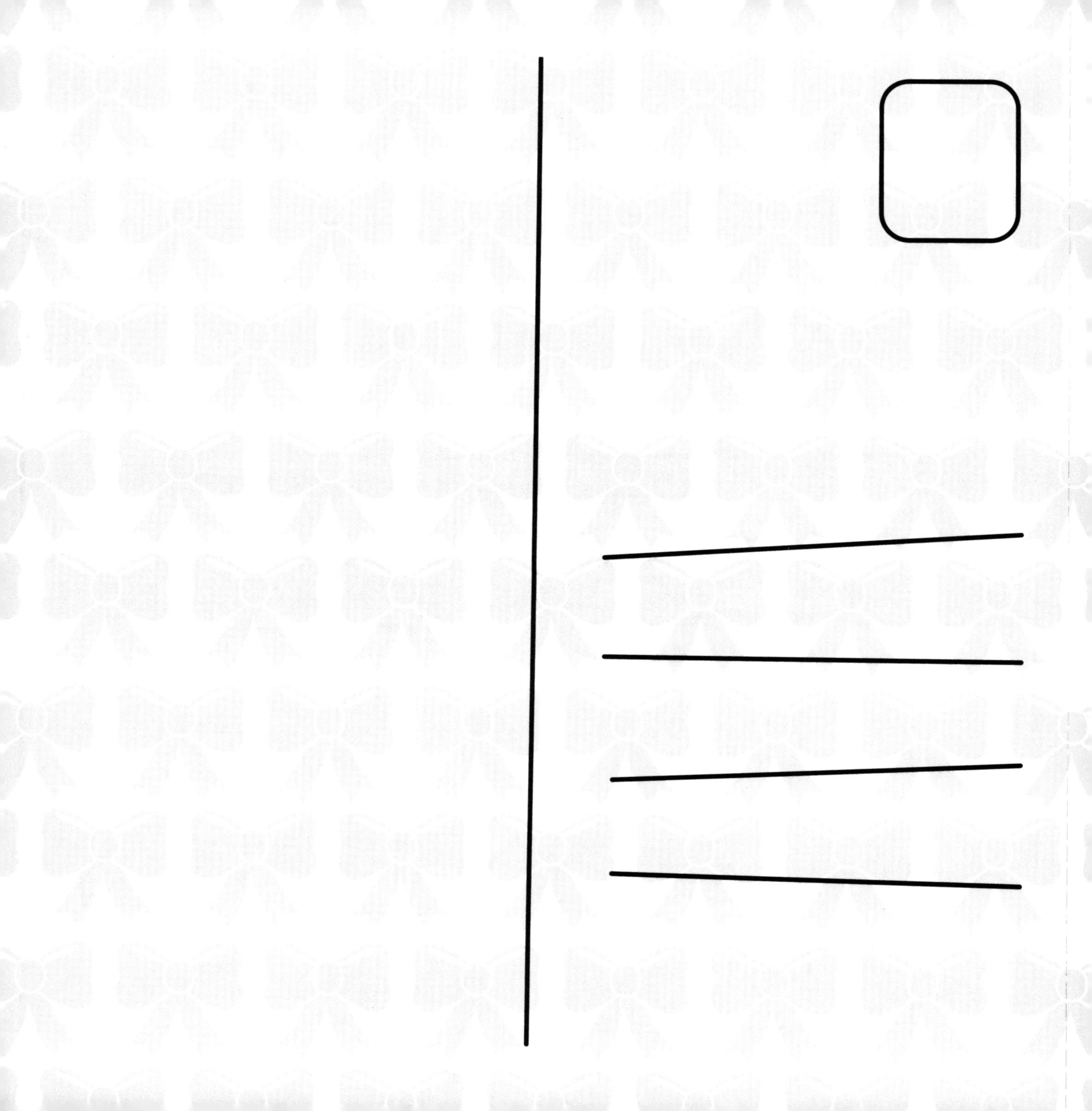

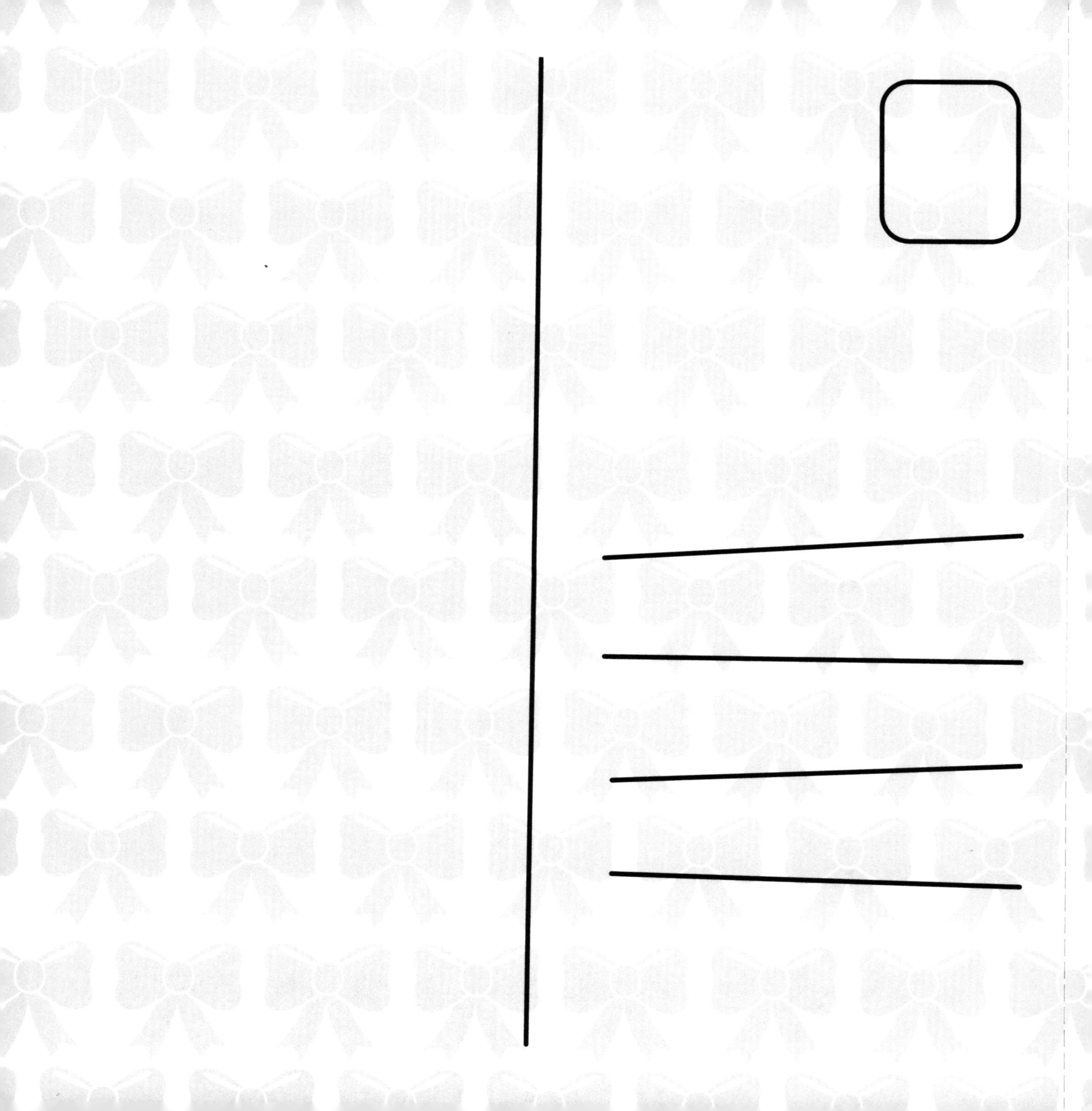

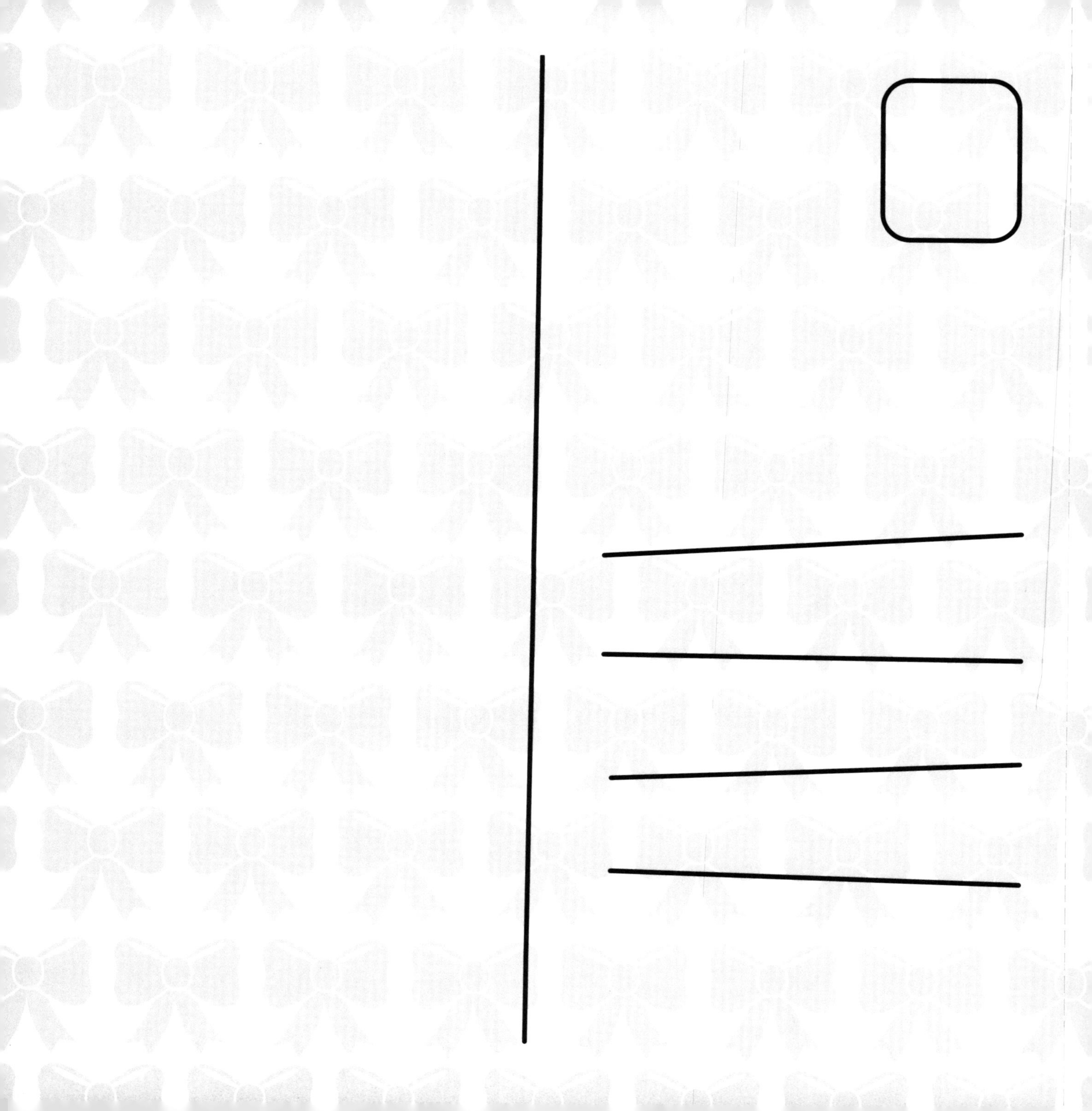

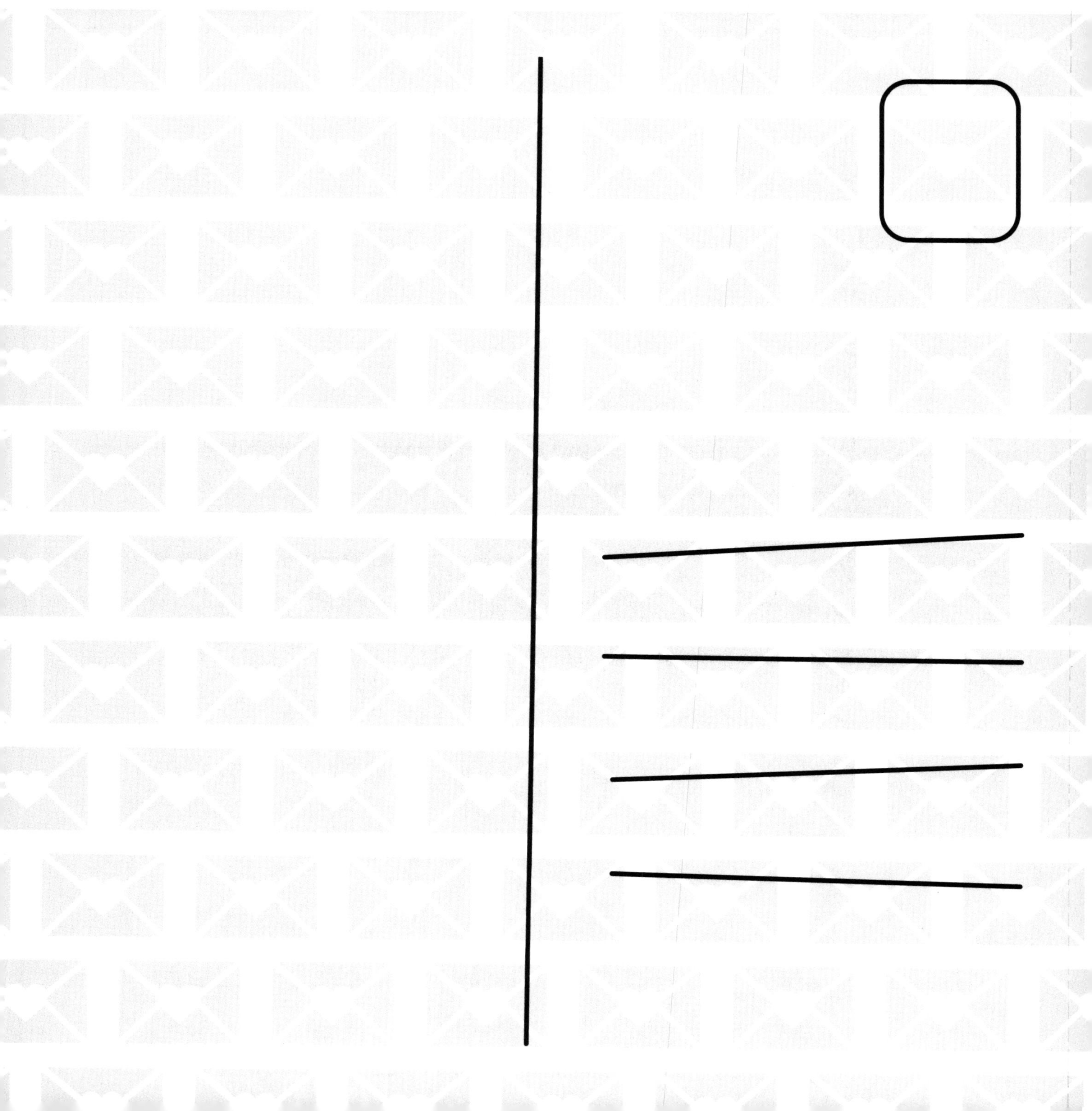

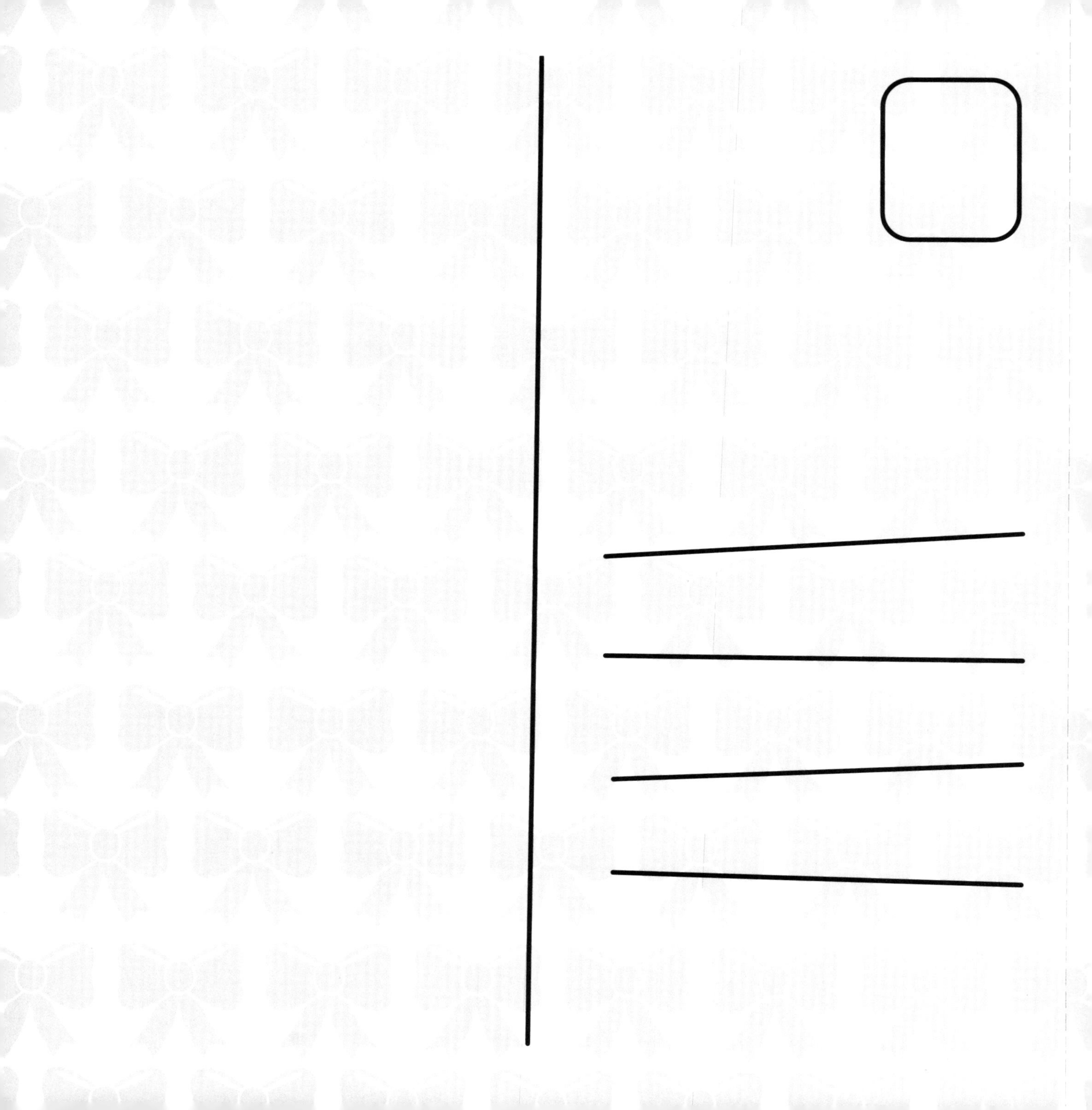

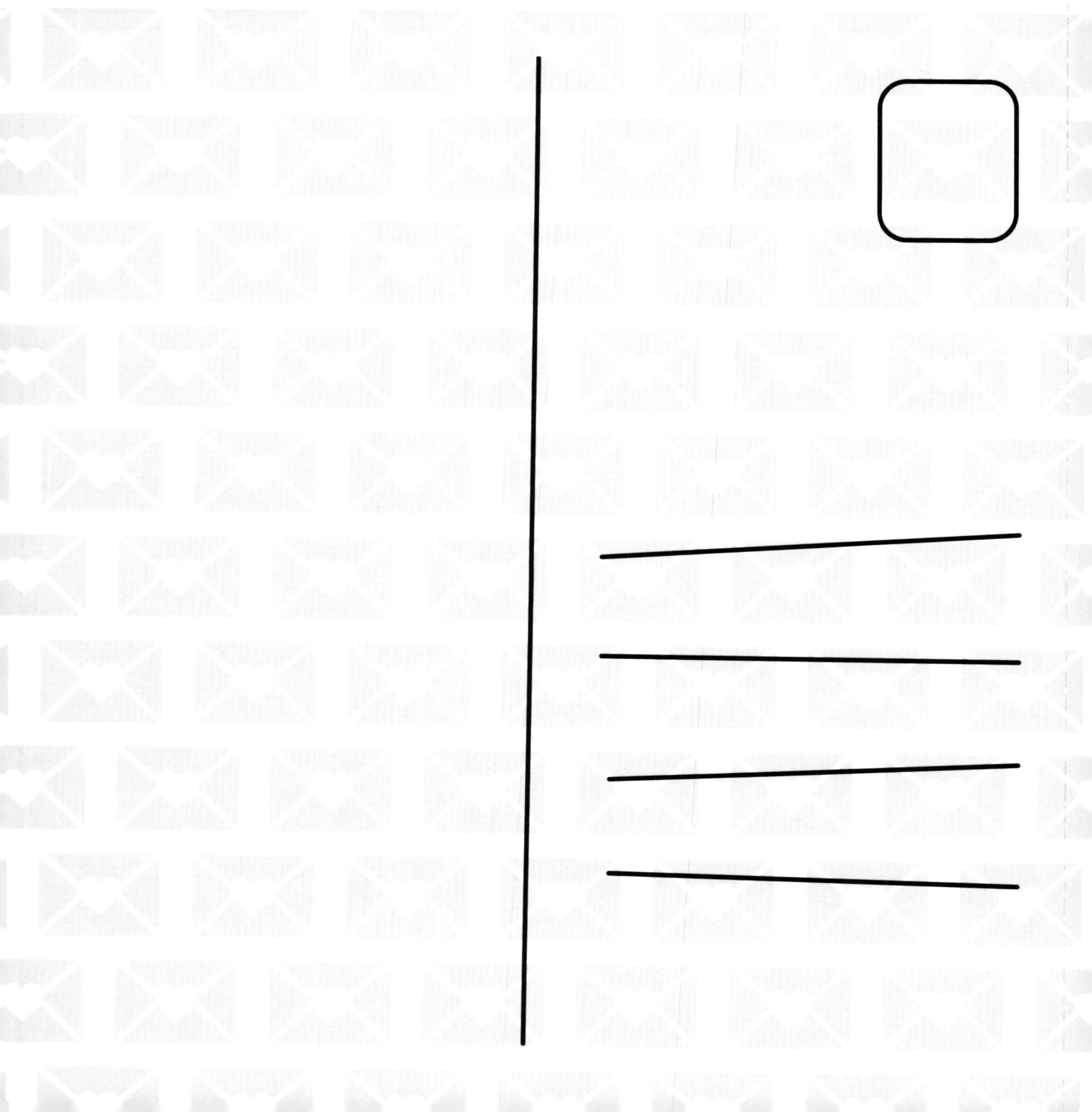

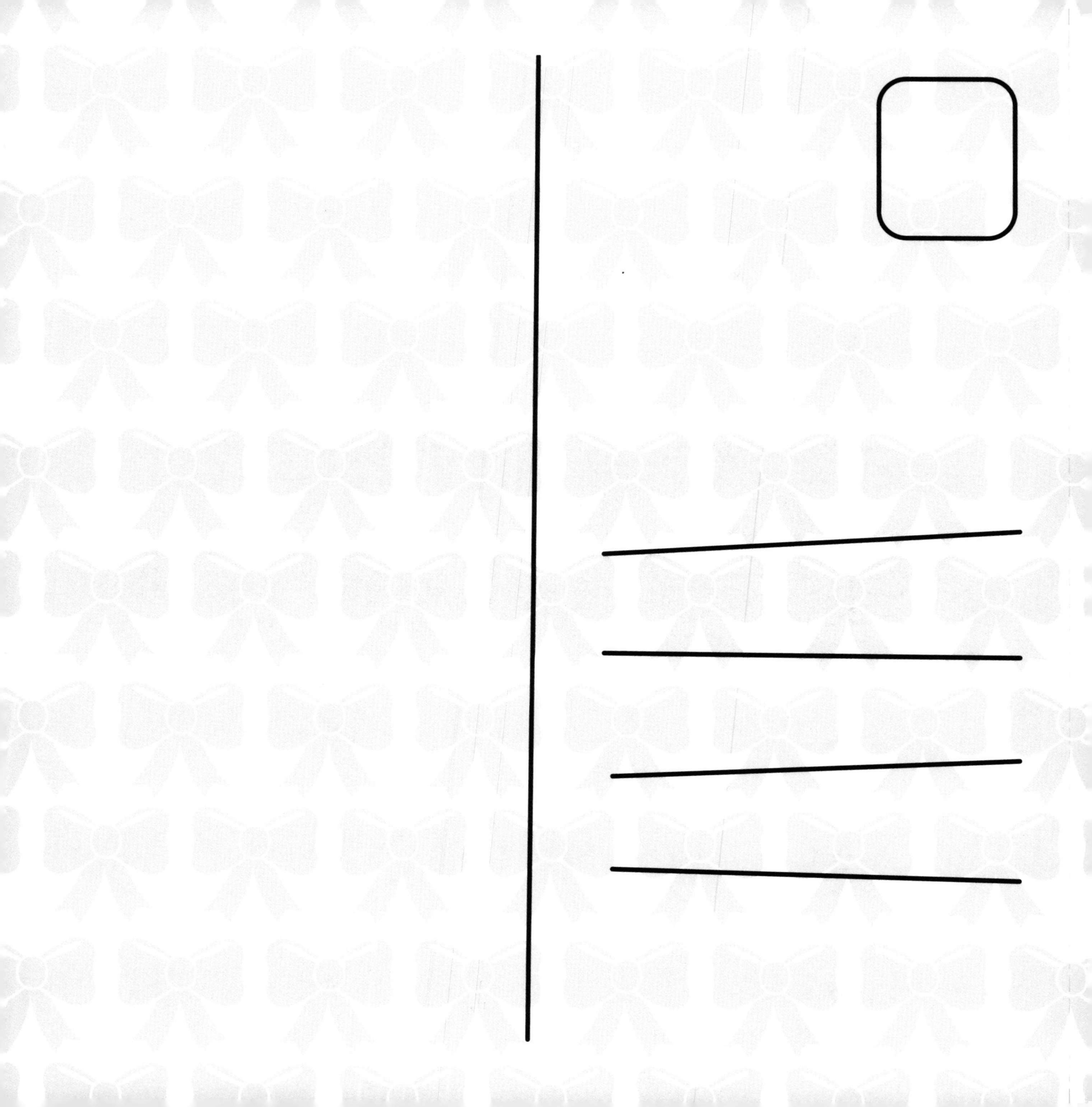

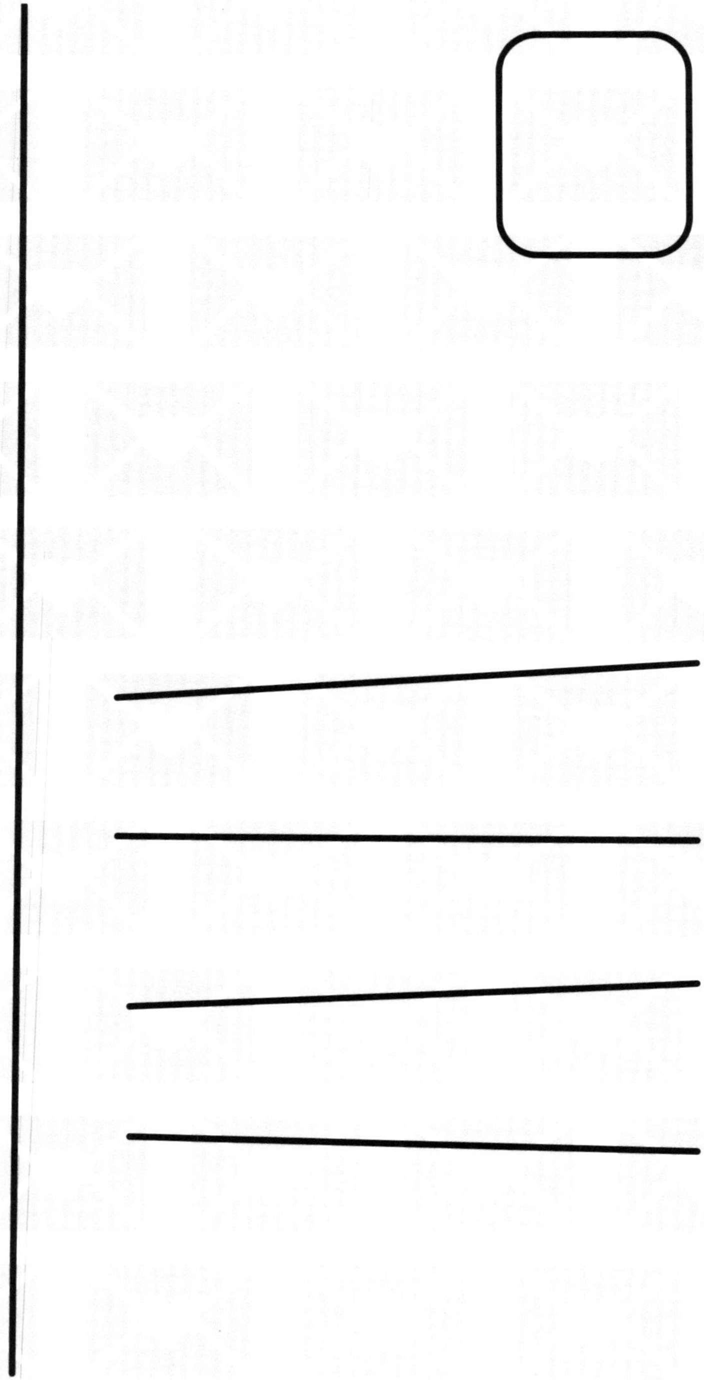

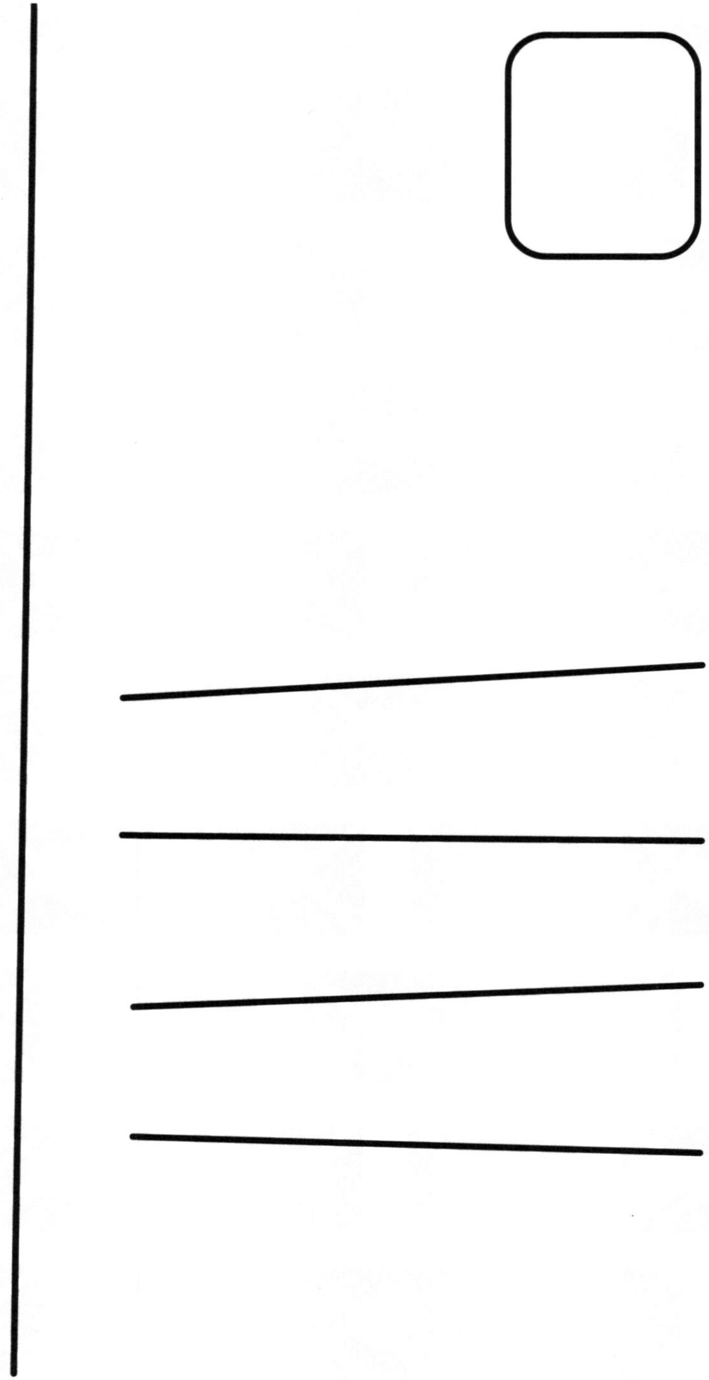

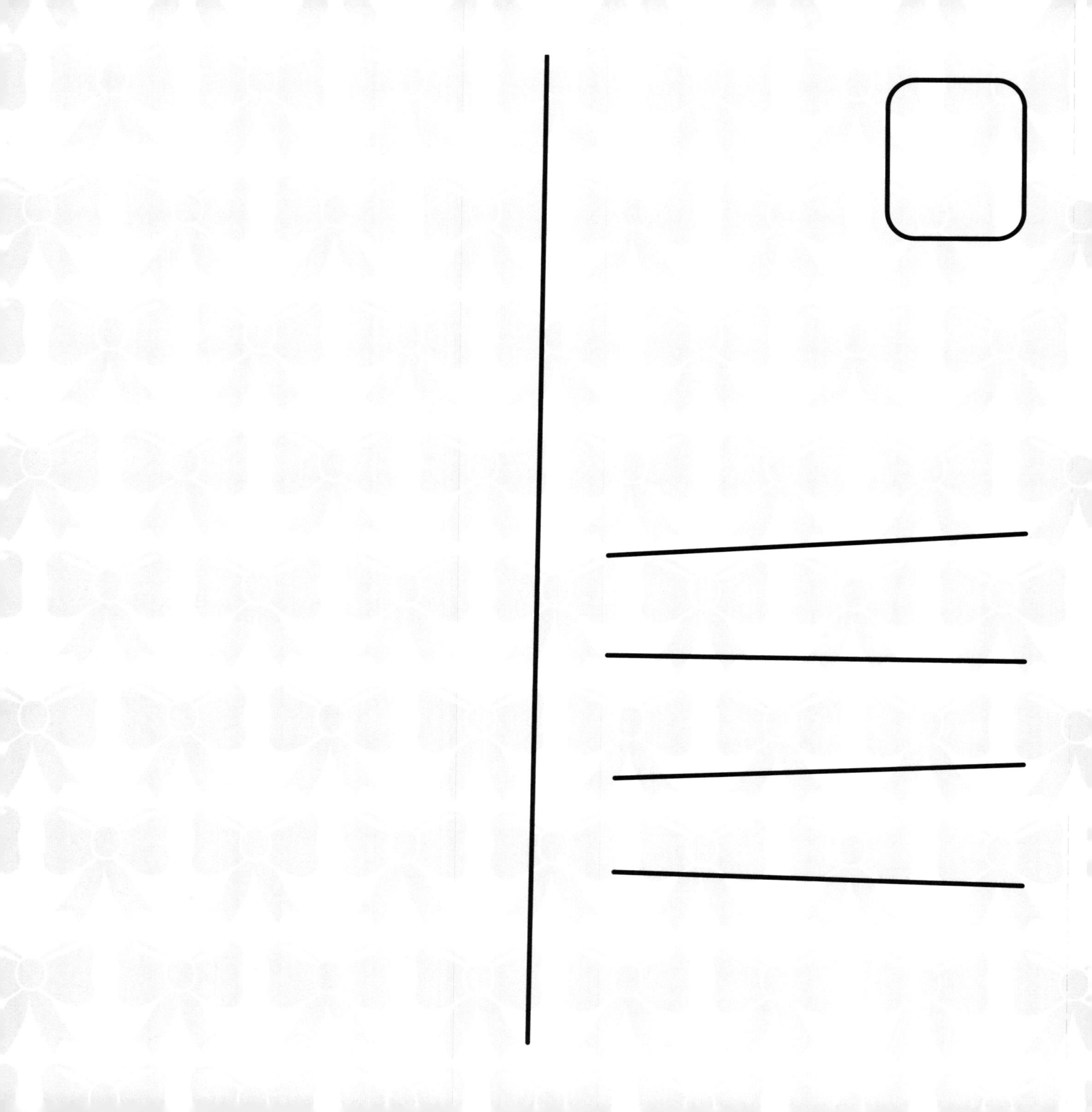

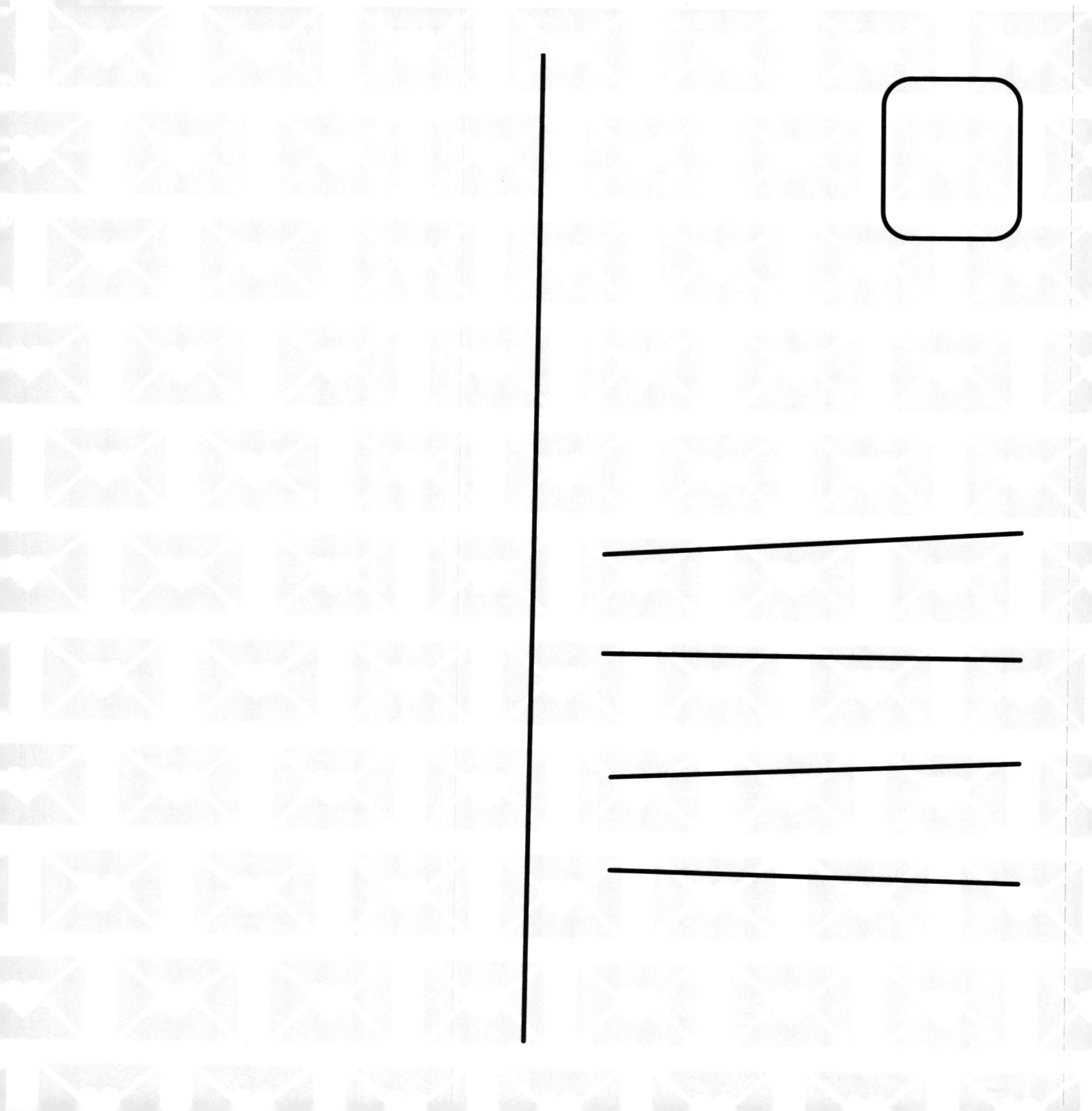

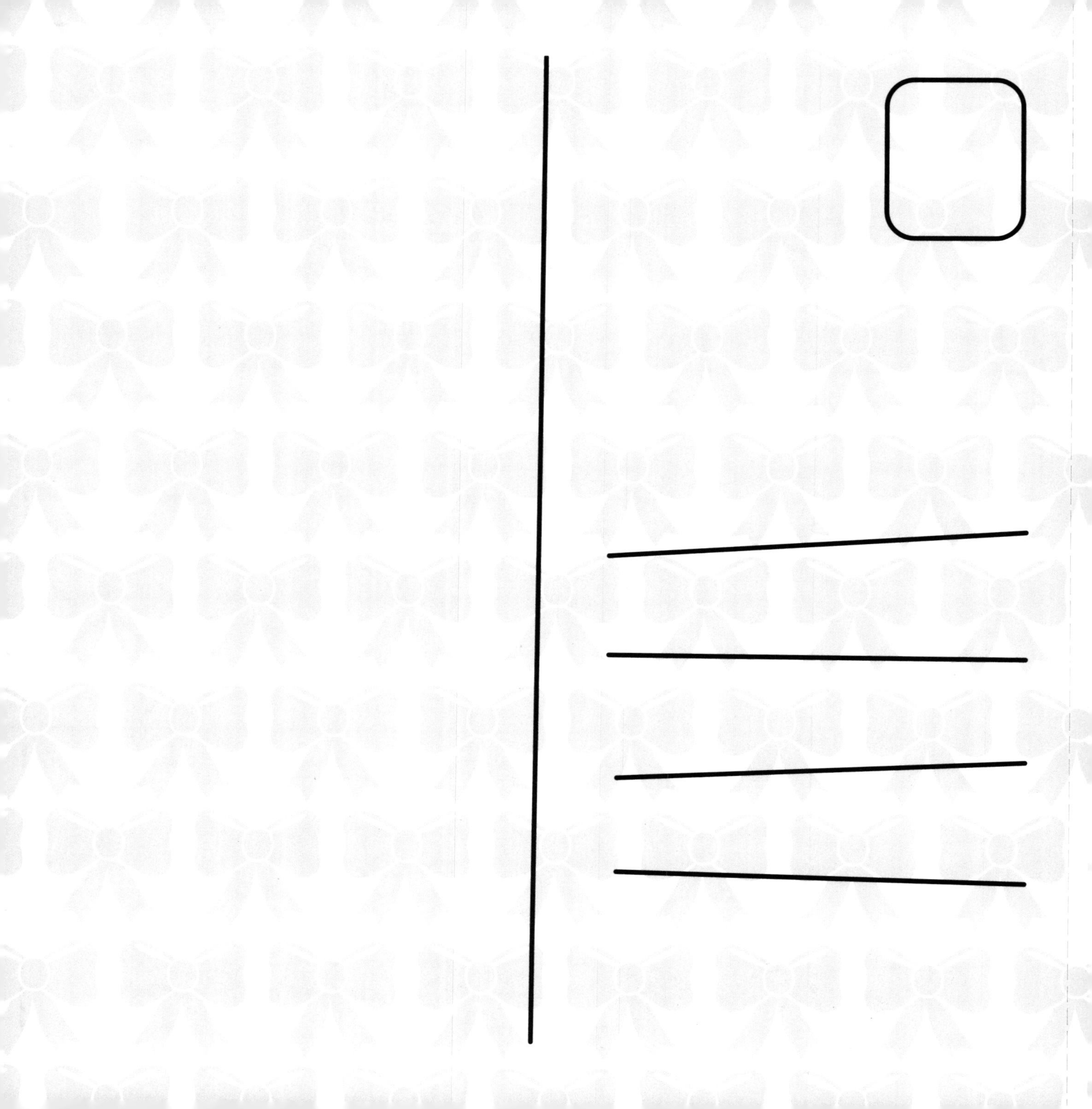

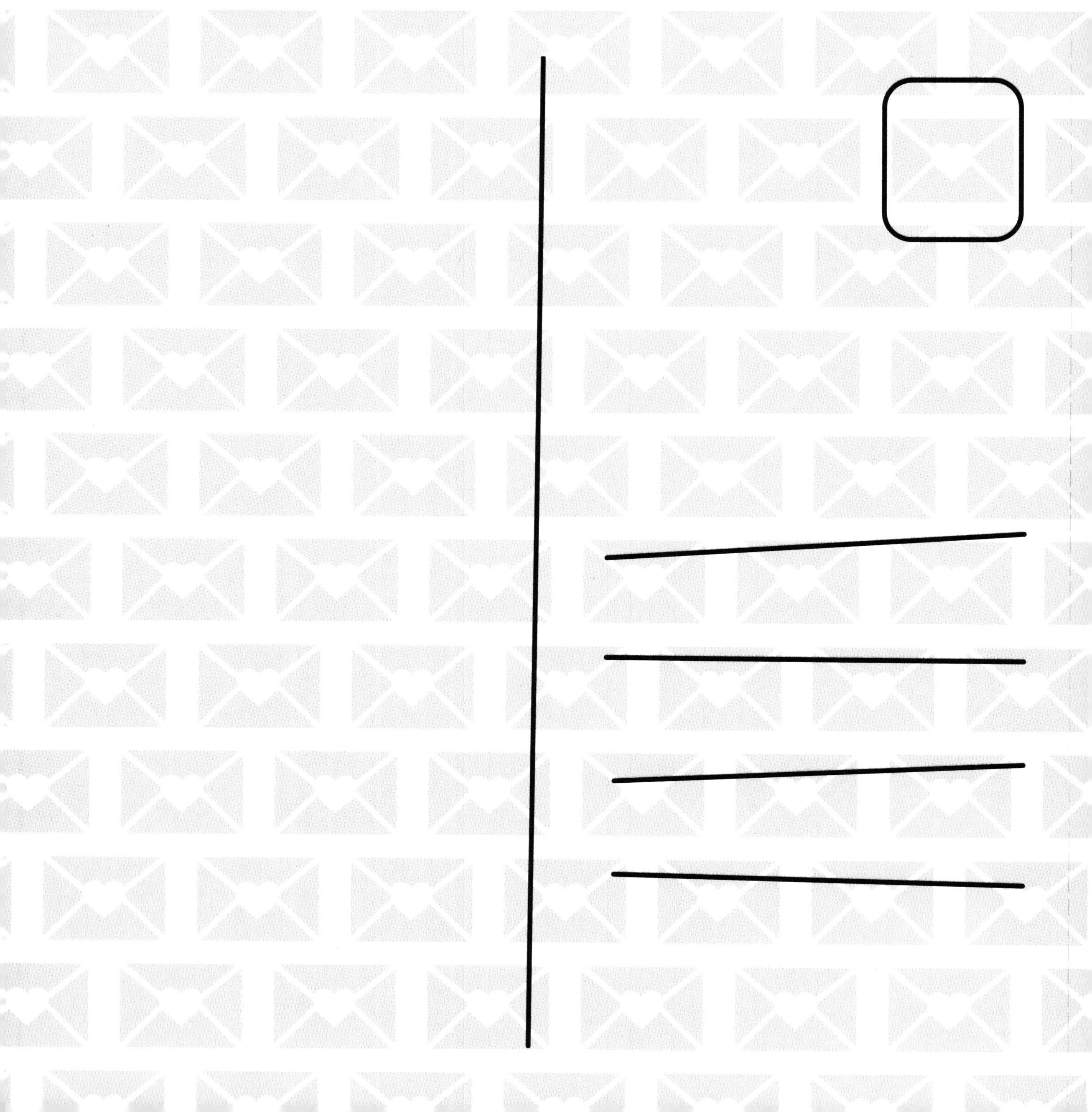